HELLO! WELCOME TO THE FABUMOUSE WORLD OF THE THEA SISTERS!

Thea Sisters

Hi, I'm Thea Stilton, Geronimo Stilton's sister! I am a special reporter for _The Rodent's Gazette_, the most famous newspaper on Mouse Island. I love traveling and meeting new mice all over the world, like the Thea Sisters. These five friends have helped me out with my adventures. Let me introduce you to these fabumouse young mice!

Colette has a real passion for fashion. She loves to design her own clothes in her favorite color, pink.

Violet loves studying and learning new things. She is a fan of classical music and dreams of becoming a famouse violinist someday.

Pamela loves pizza so much she eats it for breakfast. She is a skilled mechanic who can fix just about any motor she gets her paws on.

PAULINA is shy and loves to read about faraway places. But she loves traveling to those places even more.

Nicky is from the Australian Outback, where she developed a love of nature and the environment. This outdoors-loving mouse is always on the move.

Thea Sisters

Thea Stilton

MOUSEFORD ACADEMY

THE FRIENDSHIP RECIPE

Scholastic Inc.

Copyright © 2012 by Edizioni Piemme S.p.A., Palazzo Mondadori, Via Mondadori 1, 20090 Segrate, Italy. International Rights © Atlantyca S.p.A. English translation © 2017 by Atlantyca S.p.A.

The publisher does not have any control over and does not assume any responsibility for author or third-party websites or their content.

GERONIMO STILTON and THEA STILTON names, characters, and related indicia are copyright, trademark, and exclusive license of Atlantyca S.p.A. All rights reserved. The moral right of the author has been asserted. Based on an original idea by Elisabetta Dami.

www.geronimostilton.com

Published by Scholastic Inc., *Publishers since 1920*, 557 Broadway, New York, NY 10012. SCHOLASTIC and associated logos are trademarks and/or registered trademarks of Scholastic Inc.

Stilton is the name of a famous English cheese. It is a registered trademark of the Stilton Cheese Makers' Association. For more information, go to www.stiltoncheese.com.

This book is a work of fiction. Names, characters, places, and incidents are either the product of the author's imagination or are used fictitiously, and any resemblance to actual persons, living or dead, business establishments, events, or locales is entirely coincidental.

ISBN 978-1-338-18274-3

Text by Thea Stilton
Original title *La ricetta dell'amicizia*
Cover by Giuseppe Facciotto
Illustrations by Barbara Pellizzari (pencils) and Francesco Castelli (color)
Graphics by Chiara Cebraro

Special thanks to Shannon Penney
Translated by Anna Pizzelli
Interior design by Becky James

10 9 8 7 6 5 4 3 2 1   17 18 19 20 21

Printed in the U.S.A.   40
First printing 2017

HEADMASTER IN THE KITCHEN!

One sunny afternoon, Octavius de Mousus, the headmaster of Mouseford Academy, was taking a break to watch his favorite cooking show, Healthy Nibbles with Chef Crouton! It was a famouse TV competition for amateur chefs, hosted by the one and only Chef Crouton — the most mousetastic cook around.

That day, the headmaster learned the secret to baking a perfect soufflé: never open the oven door before the cooking time is over. Otherwise, the rising soufflé will deflate like a balloon! Holey cheese!

Hello!

The recipe of the day was cheddar soufflé, and the one Chef Crouton was baking looked fabumouse! The headmaster couldn't help himself — that NIGHT, after the students were all back in their rooms, he SNUCK into the academy's kitchen to bake a soufflé of his own.

"Pawsome patience is the secret to success!" de Mousus hummed to himself, imitating Chef Crouton as he checked his soufflé through the oven door.

The soufflé was rising and looking mousetastically *delicious*. Yum! Just then the headmaster's thoughts were interrupted by a loud sound.

RINNNNNNNG!

Squeak! The ringing sound must have been the oven timer!

"It's ready!" the headmaster cried.

He rushed to OPEN the oven door — and the soufflé deflated. **RATS!**

RINNNNNNNG!

The headmaster suddenly understood. The ringing wasn't coming from the oven — it was coming from his **CELL PHONE**!

"Hello?" he answered the call, *frazzled*.

"Hello, this is **CHEF CROUTON**!" a familiar voice squeaked on the other end of the line.

"Am I speaking to Headmaster de Mousus? I apologize for calling so late."

Thundering cattails! The headmaster couldn't believe his ears — he was squeaking with his favorite chef!

"Ch-chef C-crouton?" the headmaster squeaked. "REALLY?!"

"Yes," Chef Crouton went on. "I'm calling because I received your letter."

A month ago, the headmaster had written a long letter to Chef Crouton, inviting him to teach a class at Mouseford Academy about preparing healthy, tasty food. He knew that the students would love it — and they'd learn a lot, too!

"I would be delighted to teach the Mouseford students everything I know!" CHEF CROUTON said agreeably.

Cheese and crackers, what fabumouse luck!

The chef wasn't going to waste a moment — he planned to arrive the very next day! After hanging up his phone, the headmaster quickly dumped his deflated soufflé in the garbage and headed home as fast as his paws would take him. He had a cheeseload of planning to do!

A WELCOME GUEST — OR TWO?

News spreads quickly at Mouseford, and the next morning, Chef Crouton's arrival was all anyone could squeak about.

"Can you believe it?" Nicky cried. "A class taught by one of the most famouse chefs in the world!"

"I've learned a lot just from watching his **TV show**," Violet said. "For example, you should always choose your ingredients according to what's in season."

Colette chimed in, "I learned there are ways to make your food not only healthy and delicious, but **pink**, too — like mixing diced strawberries into your oatmeal!"

"If you paired it with salmon and some

beet salad, you'd have your ultimate day of completely pink meals!" Paulina joked.

The Thea Sisters all burst out laughing. Then each one of them started describing their favorite foods: Paulina liked fresh, colorful veggies paired with different tasty dips; Nicky loved high-energy foods like peanut-butter-and-banana sandwiches on whole-wheat bread; and Violet enjoyed pairing different dishes with the perfect teas.

"Pam, what's your favorite meal?" Violet asked with a wink. "Let me guess:

PERFECTLY PINK MEALS

OATMEAL WITH DICED STRAWBERRIES

GRILLED SALMON

BEET SALAD

PIZZA for every course?"

When no one squeaked up, the Thea Sisters all **LOOKED** at one another, confused. Where was Pam?

Colette thought for a minute. "When I left our room, she was on the phone."

What Pam's friends didn't know was that Pam had been squeaking with her brother Vince. He was planning to *visit* Mouseford in a few days!

"Guess what?!" Pam exclaimed then, bursting into the room. "I have mouserific news — a guest is coming!"

"We already know all about it," Paulina replied, assuming her friend was talking about **CHEF CROUTON**.

Pam's jaw dropped. "How is that possible? I just **FOUND OUT** a few minutes ago!"

Colette shrugged. "While you were on the phone, we all read the announcement on the message board."

What announcement? There was an announcement about her brother's visit? Pam ran to the message board . . . and burst out laughing. She and her friends were talking about totally different visitors!

"Sorry," she announced. "I guess two guests are arriving: Chef Crouton and my brother Vince!"

THE LESSON IS SERVED!

That afternoon, a large crowd gathered in the Great Hall. Everybody was eager to find out exactly what **CHEF CROUTON'S** class was going to be all about . . . everybody except Pam.

"I really don't understand why everyone's got their tails in a twist over a class about *healthy eating*," she said, sitting down next to her friends. "**YUCK!**"

"What's so **GROSS** about eating healthy foods?" Nicky asked, raising an eyebrow.

Pam rolled her eyes. "We're talking about food with no taste . . . *boring*!" she squeaked, pulling a buttered everything bagel from her backpack.

GRANOLA AND YOGURT

"How can you be so sure that **HEALTHY** food doesn't taste good, too?" Nicky asked her. "I'll bet your bagel isn't any yummier than my **granola and yogurt**!"

Just then Chef Crouton himself interrupted their conversation! He entered the Great Hall pushing a **CART** that carried two **MYSTERIOUS** plates of food.

"Hello, everybody!" he said with a smile. "I'm Chef Crouton, and I'm here to teach you how to prepare fun and delicious food that's also nutritious! I always say it should be **yummy AND good for your tummy**. Now, I need a volunteer!"

Lots of 🐾🐾🐾🐾 went up, but a small group of mouselets caught Chef Crouton's attention — Colette, Violet, Nicky, and Paulina, who were secretly *pointing* to Pam as a volunteer!

Intrigued, Chef Crouton called Pam up and showed her what was on the two mystery plates.

"I prepared some French fries and a baked sweet potato," he explained. "Could you try them both and tell me which one is tastier?"

Pick her!

Hee, hee, hee!

Huh?

Hmm . . . her!

Let's start with a taste test!

"The French fries will win," Pam said with a shrug, "but if you **REALLY** want me to taste both dishes . . ."

As soon as she took a bite of the **first** French fry, Pam was sure she was right. It was fabumouse!

But when she tried the baked sweet potato, she was almost squeakless. It was delicious . . . marvemouse, in fact!

"This baked sweet potato is **UNBEATABLE**!" she cried.

While Pam kept munching on the potato, Chef Crouton turned to the other students

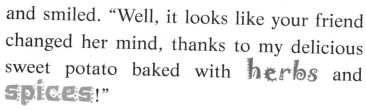

and smiled. "Well, it looks like your friend changed her mind, thanks to my delicious sweet potato baked with herbs and spices!"

Pam grinned, helping herself to another forkful. She had to admit, maybe Nicky was right — healthy food could be TASTY, too!

A VERY SPECIAL CLASS

Chef Crouton **loved** teaching things the way he had learned them himself — paws-on!

As a young mouselet, he had **traveled** to every corner of the world to learn about different kinds of food. In Italy, he had learned how to make fresh pasta; in Norway, how to smoke sardines; in **India**, how to use spices. He hadn't ever gone to a traditional **cooking school**.

Because of his experiences, he decided to take his students on food-related **ADVENTURES** of their own!

In order to teach the students the importance of shopping **LOCALLY** for their food, Chef Crouton led the class on

FRESH PASTA

SPICES

SMOKED SARDINES

a trip to a honey farm on Whale Island. The honey was harvested right there by a beekeeper and his family, so it was fresh and d*elicious*!

To teach his students how to plan **NUTRITIOUS MEALS**, he took them straight to Mouseford's enormouse pantry. There, he demonstrated how to create a meal with the right balance of fruits, vegetables, proteins, and carbohydrates.

Finally, Chef Crouton took the class to the local farmers' market. He wanted his students to understand the importance of eating local, seasonal produce, which is fresher and often tastier because it doesn't have to travel as far before it's purchased. There, the chef demonstrated how to use all five senses when picking out fresh fruits and vegetables.

Show me the fruit that's in season!

A Season for All Fruit

SPRING

kiwis, apricots, lemons, limes, cherries, peas, radishes, green beans

SUMMER

watermelons, melons, peaches, raspberries, blueberries, strawberries, blackberries, cucumbers, eggplant, onions, peppers

FALL

pears, grapes, chestnuts, pomegranates, oranges, fennel, sweet potatoes, mushrooms, cabbages, beets, squashes, turnips

WINTER

clementines, grapefruit, artichokes, cauliflower, broccoli, cabbages, leeks, pears

The Thea Sisters' eating habits were getting better and better each day, thanks to the chef's suggestions and **tips**.

Violet found out that using local **HONEY** instead of processed sugar made her tea taste even more delicious.

Nicky learned that eating a **banana** before a run gave her more energy and improved her workouts.

Colette discovered that choosing **BETTER** ingredients even helped her beauty routine. Who knew that **olive oil** made such a fabumouse lip balm?

Paulina started adding nuts to her **salads** to make her meals more **nutritious** and **filling**.

But the Thea

sister who was getting the most out of the class was Pam. She wasn't giving up her favorite foods, but she was learning to KEEP AN OPEN MIND and taste different things — even if they weren't foods she would normally TRY!

On the other paw, there was one mouse who thought that Chef Crouton's class was boring and useless: Ruby Flashyfur!

Ruby complained during the long walk to the market. "I can't take Chef Crouton and his babbling about nutrition anymore. I can't wait for this class to be over!"

But Ruby didn't know that Chef Crouton still had a cheeseload of SURPRISES in store for the Mouseford students . . .

CHEF CROUTON'S TEN RULES FOR HEALTHY EATING

1. Always eat fruits and vegetables.
2. Drink lots of water throughout the day.
3. Avoid sugary drinks and limit sugary foods.
4. Don't eat too many fatty or fried foods.
5. Choose in-season, local produce.
6. Don't eat too much.
7. Start your day with a healthy, balanced breakfast — it will give you energy!
8. Chew slowly — you'll be able to enjoy the taste of your food more!
9. Get plenty of exercise.
10. Keep trying foods you think you don't like. You might change your mind!

Remember: It should be yummy AND good for your tummy!

GUESTS AND UNEXPECTED NEWS

The days went by faster than a mouse on a cheese hunt, and soon it was time for Chef Crouton to leave Mouseford Academy. While he was packing, he couldn't stop thinking about his students' enthusiasm. They had learned so much in just a few weeks! As he closed his last bag, he had a mousetastic idea! Without a moment to waste, he scurried to the headmaster's office.

As soon as he walked in, he squeaked, "I'm positive that your students' enthusiasm for healthy eating would be inspiring to mouselets everywhere. I'd like them to be on my TV show!"

The headmaster scratched his snout,

perplexed. "Well, I'm sure they would be **thrilled**, but I'm afraid they'd miss too many classes . . ."

"Don't worry about that!" Chef Crouton **interrupted**. "The students won't come to the TV show — the **TV show** will come to Mouseford!"

Chef Crouton quickly explained his plan. He would **HOLD** a paws-on cooking class for a small group of students so only the ones truly interested in cooking would sign up. Those students would be featured in a special episode of *Healthy Nibbles with Chef Crouton!*

Here's my plan!

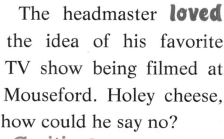

The headmaster **loved** the idea of his favorite TV show being filmed at Mouseford. Holey cheese, how could he say no?

Smiling, Chef Crouton headed for the door. "You can make the announcement, and I'll go unpack!"

At that very moment, a mouselet with curly brown hair stepped off the ferry at Whale Island's port. He carried a big backpack on his shoulders, and he looked around curiously.

"Vince!" Pam shouted, running to **hug** her brother. "I'm so excited to see you!"

"It's mousetastic to see you, too!" **Vince** replied, wrapping Pam in a big hug. He had really missed his little sister! Even though

they had an **ENORMOUSE** family, their happy home in New York wasn't the same without Pam.

"I can't wait to show you around Mouseford!" Pam squeaked, climbing into her **CAR**. "I have so much to *tell* you, so many places to SHOW you, and so many mouselets for you to meet!"

PAM AND VINCE'S PARENTS

Pam wasn't joking! In fact, as soon as they arrived at the academy, she took Vince on a whirlwind tour of the place that she lovingly called her new home.

Vince had a great time catching up with

the Thea Sisters, whom he had met once in New York. He also had a chance to meet some of his sister's other friends.

Vince could see that Pam had not only found a new home at Mouseford, but a new **family**, too.

Once he'd met all of Pam's friends, Vince

thought it would be a good time to paw over the *gift* he had brought Pam from New York. "So, Pam, I have a little —"

But he hadn't finished his sentence when he was interrupted by an excited squeak.

"Hey, I have marvemouse news!" Ron cried, rUNNiNg over to the Thea Sisters. "Chef Crouton has decided to stay at Mouseford and teach an actual cooking class!"

"You mean a paws-on class where we'll learn to cook his dishes?" Nicky squeaked.

"Exactly!" Ron said. "It's a once-in-a-lifetime opportunity! But we have to ENRoLL fast — the class is limited to a small number of students."

"HOLEY CHEESE, THAT'S FABUMOUSE!" Pam exclaimed. "Let's go sign up!"

As everyone scurried away, Pam turned

back to Vince. "I'm sorry, were you about to say something before?"

Seeing how **excited** Pam was about the new class, Vince decided to let her go. He'd give her the gift later! He grinned. "Nothing important, now go sign up for that class!"

Thanks!

A SURPRISE ANNOUNCEMENT

Many students scrambled to sign up for **CHEF CROUTON'S** class, but there was only space for twelve. The chef planned to announce the names of the lucky students that afternoon in the cafeteria. What no one knew was that he'd also reveal that they would be participating in an episode of his **TV show**!

"Hello, everyone!" the chef exclaimed through a bullhorn. "I have an **important** announcement."

The cafeteria fell silent.

ENROLLED IN THE CLASS.doc

NIBBLES

students enrolled in the
COOKING CLASS:

CRAIG, SHEN, RYDER,
RON, ELLY, TANJA,
CONNIE, COLETTE,
VIOLET, NICKY,
PAULINA, PAM

"I have here a list of the STUDENTS who will be in my cooking class."

The mouselets all burst into applause as the chef read the names. The only one who wasn't celebrating was Ruby.

"Why in the name of cheese did you even think of signing up for a class like that?" she squeaked to her friend Connie. "The Ruby Crew doesn't get our paws DIRTY cooking — we have someone do it FOR US!"

Connie was about to say that she had enjoyed Chef Crouton's class, when a voice from the bullhorn rang out again.

"One more thing,"

What did you get yourself into?

Huh?

Chef Crouton said with a smile. "In addition to the cooking class, the selected students will be featured in a *special episode* of my TV show, to be filmed right here at Mouseford!"

"**What?** We're going to be on a TV show?" Pam squeaked. "Vince! Can you even believe it?"

Vince hugged his sister. **CHEERS** echoed around the cafeteria. Cheese and crackers, everyone was so excited!

Ruby blinked in disbelief. Her classmates were going to be on a famouse TV show? Without her? *IMPAWSSIBLE!* Ruby Flashyfur was born to be in front of the camera!

LET THE COMPETITION BEGIN!

"Give up my place in the class?" Connie said to Ruby. "Not for all the cheese on Mouse Island!"

After DINNER, the two mouselets had gone back to their room. There, Ruby wasted no time asking her friend to step aside so Ruby could have her spot in the class instead.

Hearing Connie's answer, Ruby stormed out of the room, squeakless. She was used to getting what she wanted. But Ruby came back a little while later with a huge smile on her snout. She had a plan!

To get what she wanted from Connie,

Ruby knew she would have to offer her friend something she **DESPERATELY** wanted in return. So Ruby had called her mother, Rebecca Flashyfur. Within minutes, Mrs. Flashyfur had managed to snag a pass to a sold-out **rock festival**.

"Did you ever get a ticket for that music festival over the summer?" Ruby asked Connie.

"I tried," her friend replied with a sigh, "but it's been sold out for ages."

"Oh, really?" Ruby asked. "Well, I just happened to get my paws on a **PASS**! Can you believe it?"

As expected, Ruby's plan worked like a charm. The next morning, one of the students didn't show up to the first class.

"Wait, where's Connie?" Paulina asked, looking around.

"I don't know, but it's STRANGE that she's late," Violet replied. "That's not like her."

"I know — LAST NIGHT, she could hardly wait for class!" Nicky added.

Just then, **CHEF CROUTON** entered the room and cleared his throat. "Good morning, class! As you know, my show is a cooking competition. Since there are **SO MANY** of you, I thought we could divide up into teams."

The **first** team was made up of Pam, Nicky, and Paulina; the **second** team was Craig, Ron, and Tanja; and the **third** was Ryder, Elly, and Violet.

"Excuse me!" Colette squeaked, waving a paw in the air. "It looks like the **fourth** team should be Connie, Shen, and me — but Connie isn't here!"

"Your teammate has **DROPPED OUT**, unfortunately, but she sent a friend to take her place," Chef Crouton replied.

They heard **pawsteps** in the hallway . . . and there was Ruby, wearing an apron!

"Ruby?" Colette exclaimed, SURPRISED. "What are you doing here?"

"I love cooking!" Ruby replied, crossing her arms.

"Since when?" Shen asked.

"Since forever!" Ruby squeaked. "My *signature dish* is the lentil, uh, meringue. You know, the one that's marinated, er, I mean steamed in the oven!"

Shen and Colette looked at each other, worried to the tips of their whiskers. Ruby knew NOTHING about cooking — and now she was on their team!

CONSTRUCTION TIME

Chef Crouton's cooking competition involved **four rounds**. The team that won each round would earn a point, and the team with the most points at the end of all four rounds would Win the competition. The cooking was going to take place in the fully equipped TV studio that the chef and his team were setting up at Mouseford.

But — **squeak!** — building a TV set was no easy task! Whale Island was suddenly **taken over** by technicians and stagehands working day and night.

The set of *Healthy Nibbles with Chef Crouton: Mouseford Special* was being built inside a large hall at Mouseford. The

Thea Sisters jumped in snout-first to help out!

Pam offered to **ESCORT** the set decorator around the island, and Vince came along, too. She was excited to share this *fun*, **unusual** experience with her big brother!

Even though he was having a good time, Vince couldn't help feeling like Pam was awfully busy and distracted. Between the excitement of the show, her regular schoolwork, and learning paws-on cooking skills with Chef Crouton to get ready for the competition, she was always running off to do something! **RATS!**

ON THE AIR

Finally, the big day arrived. The show was going **on the air**! The Thea Sisters and their teammates walked into the TV studio, which was **glowing** with bright stage lights.

"**WOW!**" Violet exclaimed. "I can't believe they put together a TV studio complete with real **kitchens** in such a short time!"

"I know," Paulina agreed, looking around in awe. "Just think — pretty soon, we'll get to cook right here under these **LIGHTS**!"

"I hope we can remember

everything Chef Crouton has been teaching us," Craig squeaked nervously. "I don't want to look like a **CHEESEBRAIN** on TV!"

At that moment, a young mouse approached, carrying a **BOX** in his paws.

"Hello, everyone!" he squeaked. "My name is Tom, and I'm going to help direct you during filming. These are for you!"

He handed out **colorful** aprons.

These are for you!

Appearance is everything!

"Oops, is there an extra?" Tom asked, holding one last apron after all the students had put theirs on.

"No, that one is for Ruby," Colette explained. "She'll be here as soon as she's done with hair and makeup." Colette rolled her eyes and pointed to where Ruby was busy primping like the STAR of the show.

Once Ruby was finally finished, the whole group followed Tom to their places on the set. How mouserifically exciting! The lights were blinding, and the students' paws were shaking. Pam was the

most nervous of all — she couldn't help wondering if she would **really** be able to prepare healthy dishes.

TWEEEEEEEET!

An unmistakable *whistle* distracted Pam — it was Vince! He sat in the audience, waving and nodding in encouragement. A grin stretched across Pam's snout as the director announced, "Everybody ready? Three, two, one: *on the air*!"

Go, Pam!

The audience burst into a round of **applause** as Chef Crouton stepped onto the set. He greeted everyone, explained how the competition would work, and then introduced the teams.

Backstage, Headmaster de Mousus was

GETTING READY to go on. Chef Crouton had insisted that the headmaster announce the first cooking round.

"Good morning, Chef Crouton, and good morning to you, home viewers," de Mousus repeated over and over again under his breath. The poor headmaster's whiskers were wobbling with nerves! "Good—"

Just then, he heard Chef Crouton call his name. "And now let's welcome Mouseford Academy's headmaster, Octavius de Mousus!"

CLAP! CLAP! CLAP! CLAP!
CLAP! CLAP! CLAP! CLAP!
CLAP! CLAP! CLAP! CLAP!

Once he stepped in front of the cameras, Headmaster de Mousus was even more **nervous** than before! **Squeak!**

"Um . . . good morning, home chef, and good morning, audience Crouton!"

Chef Crouton grinned and winked at the cameras. "The headmaster is mousetastically *funny*, isn't he? But now let's get this competition started with the first round: grocery shopping!"

Welcome, Headmaster de Mousus!

Um . . .

TO THE MARKET, EVERYONE!

For the **first round** of the competition, Chef Crouton explained that the teams would each have thirty minutes to choose a dessert recipe and buy the **best** available ingredients. The teams had to leave the TV studio and follow the chef to Whale Island's market.

As soon as they set paw outside, Ruby walked right over to a **BRIGHT RED** van parked nearby. As she was about to climb in, Chef Crouton called after her:

"Miss Flashyfur, where do you think you're going? That van is for the film crew!"

"We're not going to walk **all the way** to the market, are we?" Ruby asked, eyes wide.

"Of course not — we'll **ride bikes**!" the chef replied, waving as the van's driver pulled away.

Behind the van, the contestants spotted four **brightly colored**, three-seater bikes — one for each team! — which they rode all the way to the market. The chef had a single-seater bike of his own to ride along with them.

Ha, ha!

This is so much fun!

"Come on, mouselets!" Chef Crouton exclaimed as he climbed off his bicycle. "Thirty minutes will go by quickly! You'll need to decide which dessert you want to make, then buy the necessary ingredients as quick as a mouse. CHefs: on your marks . . . Get set . . . Go!"

Pamela, Nicky, and Paulina (the Orange team), and Craig, Ron, and Tanja (the

Huff, huff . . .

Green team) chose their recipes quickly, and confidently ran to the market stalls. On the other paw, Violet, Ryder, and Elly (the Yellow team), and Colette, Shen, and Ruby (the Blue team) took a few more minutes to decide.

"How about a **yogurt cake**?" Ryder suggested to his teammates.

Elly thought about it for a minute. "That's a good idea, but let's pick something that would use more local ingredients."

"**HOLEY CHEESE!**" Violet exclaimed, waving a paw at the stall run by the beekeeper they had met on their field trip. "Follow me — I have an idea!"

Meanwhile, the Blue team was still discussing different **recipes**.

"We could bake something using puff pastry," Colette suggested.

"Ooh, yum! Maybe we could fill it with seasonal **FRUIT**. Apricots? Figs?" Shen asked.

"Fabumouse idea!" Colette cheered. "Let's make fig strudels with apricot jam! What do you say, Ruby?"

Ruby had been thinking about SOMETHING ELSE entirely, but she pretended to be paying attention. "Oh, yes, marvemouse idea . . . let's bake a dessert . . ."

Ruby was so busy thinking of ways to make sure the opposing teams would lose, she wasn't helping her team win!

"Okay," Colette went on, watching Ruby carefully, "we need to get the ingredients to make puff pastry, plus some good apricot jam and sweet figs."

Just then, out of the corner of her **EYE**, Ruby spotted the Green team pausing at a nearby fruit stall.

"I'll get the figs!" she squeaked. Without thinking twice, she **scurried** toward her competitors.

Let's buy peaches!

THE BEST SHOPPERS

Sneaky Ruby carried out her underpawed plan while Colette and Shen were busy looking for the best strudel ingredients. First, she made sure she wasn't being filmed. Then she moved closer to the Green team, quietly took a bag of peaches from Ron's shopping basket, and tossed it in the garbage!

"Okay, chefs!" Chef Crouton called. "Time is almost up!"

Colette glanced at Shen, worried. "We have most of the ingredients — but where is Ruby?"

"She's still at the fruit stall!" Shen replied, POINTING. "Ruby, get your tail in gear!"

Snapping to attention, Ruby glanced at

a bin of **figs** and pulled one out with her paw. "Ugh — these are so **dirty**!"

The mouse behind the stall stared at her. Had this mouselet lost her cheese? "Of course they are — they were just picked! You just have to **RINSE** them off."

"Yuck!" Ruby replied. "You know what? I'll get these instead. They look cleaner."

These figs are dirty!

Of course — they're fresh!

With that, she grabbed a package of dried figs and *caught up* with her team just in the nick of time.

The contestants headed back to the TV studio. They were all eager to hear Chef Crouton's feedback on their shopping trip!

"Welcome back," the chef said. "Now, each team can tell me which recipes you picked and show me your groceries."

The Orange team went first. "We decided to make a lemon tart," Nicky explained, "so we bought the ingredients for the crust, plus lots of fresh lemons."

"Very good," Chef Crouton said, smiling. "What about you, Green team? What did you choose to make?"

"Stuffed peaches!" Ron proudly replied.

"Uh-oh!" Tanja squeaked as she and Craig placed their groceries on the counter. "We have an enormouse problem — the peaches **AREN'T HERE**!"

Where are the peaches?

The members of the Green team were sure that they had bought the *peaches*, but Chef Crouton explained that only the groceries that made it back to the studio would count.

"You'll make it up in the **next round**!" he said.

Seeing that her plan was **WORKING**, Ruby smiled. When Colette began telling the chef about their dessert, Ruby could already *taste* their victory.

"Fig and apricot strudel?" Chef Crouton said. "Marvemouse!

"But it's TOO BAD you picked dried figs," the chef went on, inspecting their ingredients. "Right now, the markets are full of fresh figs. Those are much richer in **vitamins**!"

Annoyed, Ruby tried to downplay her mistake by pointing to the Yellow team. "But they bought dried fruit, too!"

Violet, Elly, and Ryder had bought eggs, butter, flour, honey, sugar, milk, hazelnuts, chocolate, vanilla bean, and dried strawberries. Ryder explained that they would use those ingredients to make crepes with homemade hazelnut-chocolate filling. The dried strawberries were a garnish, since fresh strawberries weren't in season.

"Mousetastic choice!" Chef Crouton declared with a grin. "Especially because you thought to make the **hazelnut-chocolate** filling yourself, instead of buying one ready-made. The first-round winner is the Yellow team!"

YUMMY CREPES

CREPES INGREDIENTS:
2 large eggs
1 cup flour
1 tsp vanilla extract
a sprinkle of salt
1 1/4 cups milk
2 1/2 tbs melted butter (plus more to grease the pan)

FILLING INGREDIENTS:
6 tbs dark chocolate
6 tbs finely chopped hazelnuts
1 tsp sugar
4 tbs milk
dried strawberries (or fresh, if they're in season!)

To prepare the crepes, find an adult to be assistant baker. Then beat the eggs together in a small bowl and set aside. Sift flour into a larger bowl, then mix in vanilla extract and salt. Add milk, beaten eggs, and melted butter. Mix well and let sit for thirty minutes. Warm up a nonstick frying pan and grease it with butter, then pour in a scoop of batter and spread it evenly across the pan. Cook for about a minute on each side, until it's a nice golden color. Remove the crepe from the pan and put it on a plate to cool.

For the filling, melt the chocolate in a pan. Add the chopped hazelnuts, sugar, and milk. Stir well, then refrigerate for half an hour. Spread the filling on each crepe and fold in half and then in half again. Garnish with strawberries. Yum!

ANYThING TO
WIN!

Colette squeaked with her teammates
during a break in the show. "Let's not get
discouraged," she said. "The competition
just started — we'll win the next round."

"Sure as squeaking, we'll do our best!"
Shen chimed in.

Ruby nodded. She was sure they would
win . . . for reasons her teammates didn't
even know about!

In fact, Ruby had three reasons: Alicia,
Connie, and Zoe. Ruby had sent her friends
to snoop around the studio and find out
about the next challenge before anybody
else. It was a truly underpawed move!

Alicia INVESTIGATED by hiding behind

a **CLOTHING** rack. She hoped she'd overhear Chef Crouton telling the costume designer about the next round. Unfortunately, her hiding place wasn't very good — she was found in minutes! **RATS!**

Hello?

Connie couldn't get her paws on any **useful** information, either. She tried chatting with Tom, the director of the show, **hoping** he would slip and mention something about the **NEXT** round. But while they were talking, Connie's phone rang. She answered and **absentmindedly** wandered away, leaving poor Tom **confused**.

Thankfully, Ruby knew she could count on Zoe, who had the best **plan**. She brought Chef Crouton a cold drink, compliments of Headmaster de Mousus. While she was delivering the drink, she was able to **eavesdrop** on a very interesting conversation between Chef Crouton and his assistant.

As soon as she left, Zoe pulled out her **cell phone**. "Ruby? I have some information for you!"

Here you go, Chef!

PEANUT BUTTER BOOST!

Zoe found out that each **team** would receive a basket full of food in the next round of the competition. They would have to choose the best things to eat as a snack before exercising.

Ruby was determined to use her secret information to ensure that the Yellow team **wouldn't score** another point and widen their lead. Before the rest of the mouselets entered the studio, she snuck to the back table where the four baskets were set up.

In the Yellow team's basket, Ruby swapped the labels of some healthier foods with those that weren't as healthy — mayonnaise swapped with yogurt, and light cream cheese swapped with marshmallow fluff.

"Now the Yellow team will **lose** for sure!" she whispered.

And she was right! Once the round started, Ryder declared, "My mother's personal trainer told me to eat crackers with cream cheese before working out — let's add this light cream cheese to some whole-wheat crackers."

Ha, ha, ha!

At the end of the round, Chef Crouton tasted the Yellow team's snack and exclaimed, "Holey cheese! This tastes delicious, but marshmallow fluff isn't a very healthy choice."

74

The teammates looked at one another, **baffled**. Marshmallow fluff? They had grabbed the **wrong** jar!

But Ruby's plan hadn't worked out entirely in her favor. The fruit salad her team prepared was too sugary, without enough protein to offset the sweetness. The snacks still in the running were the Orange team's banana-peanut-butter-chocolate shake and the Green team's honey-granola yogurt.

Chef Crouton scratched his snout and thought long and hard before making his

SUPER SHAKE!

INGREDIENTS: one banana, 1 1/2 cups milk, 2 tbs peanut butter, 2 tbs dark cocoa

Slice the banana and ask an adult to put it in a blender with milk, peanut butter, and cocoa. Blend together and pour in a glass. Yum — fabumouse!

decision. "We have two excellent snacks here, but I choose . . . the shake! The peanut butter gives it an extra protein boost."

While Nicky, Paulina, and Pam were happily celebrating, Vince ran up to **hug** his sister. "You were the one who thought to add peanut butter, weren't you?" he asked.

"You bet your whiskers!" Pam grinned. "I knew we needed some extra protein — and **flavor**!"

Congrats! Great idea!

TASTE AND RE-CREATE

The Yellow team had assumed the jars in their basket had been swapped by mistake, but Colette couldn't help feeling uneasy. Ruby's sly smile seemed suspicious! Colette decided to keep a close EYE on her teammate during the next round.

"This round," Chef Crouton explained later that afternoon, "is called Taste and Re-create! You'll taste my famouse super-creamy soup. Then you'll have to figure out which ingredients I used and try to prepare it yourself."

The soup was truly fabumouse, but guessing

the **ingredients** was not going to be easy cheesy.

"I think there's some onion," Shen said to his teammates. Colette nodded, not taking her **EYES** off Ruby. Chef Crouton had told the teams that the soup's yellowish color didn't come from saffron, but Ruby was still pawing through the spices. A moment later, Colette saw her hide a jar of saffron in her 🐾🐾🐾 and walk slowly over to the Orange team's workspace.

Colette was so shocked she could hardly squeak! Ruby was going to add the wrong ingredient to the Orange team's pot!

"Hey, Ruby!" Colette called out. "What's in your paw?"

Ruby's snout turned red. "NOTHING! Why?"

Colette gave her teammate a sweet smile.

"I just thought I saw you grab something. Can you come over here and help me with this?"

Ruby sighed and slipped the saffron jar back onto the spice rack, **mumbling** under her breath, "Why don't you keep your snout out of other mice's business?"

Colette pretended not to hear. She was glad she'd been able to stop her *sneaky* teammate from cheating!

At the end of the round, Chef Crouton was surprised to LEARN that all four of the teams had figured out the secret to the soup's yellowish color — **pumpkin**!

The Green team won the round, though, since they were the only ones to guess the second **Main** ingredient in the soup: shrimp!

But no one had **time** to cheer for the winning team. Instead, everyone was busy looking at Shen, who suddenly was covered in strange **red spots**.

What was wrong with Shen?

AN UNEXPECTED REACTION

A short while later, the mystery had been solved. Apparently, Shen was allergic to shrimp!

"Did Shen know about his allergy?" Pam asked Colette, who was explaining what had happened to the Thea Sisters during a break before the **fourth round**.

"No, he didn't," Colette replied, shaking her head sadly. "Luckily, the doctor said he'll be better soon, but he can't cook anymore today."

"Don't worry," Vince said, trying to make her feel better. "You and Ruby **ARE STILL** in the running!"

Colette sighed. "To be honest, I think

But that's not right!

I don't know what to do . . .

Ruby is too busy **sabotaging** the other teams to be very helpful!"

Vince and the Thea Sisters listened as Colette filled them in on Ruby's *sneaky* behavior.

"You have to say something!" Vince squeaked in **disbelief**.

Nicky nodded firmly. "Yes, you need to make her understand this won't only harm your team, it will ruin everyone's fun!"

Colette knew her friends were right, so she marched up to Ruby. "Do you realize that if you had worked with me and Shen instead of trying so hard to ruin the other teams' chances, maybe we could have won?"

Why don't you help us?

Hmph!

Ruby scoffed and stuck her snout in the air. Cheese niblets, what a stubborn mouselet!

The fourth and final round of the COMPETITION required the teams to each prepare a dish of their choice that was

delicious, healthy, *beautiful*, and FUN. As soon as Chef Crouton told them to get started, Ruby quietly squeaked to Colette, "I have an idea . . ."

Holey cheese, **maybe** she had come around after all!

The students **really** let their imaginations run wild this time! Nicky, Pam, and Paulina put mozzarella and **tomatoes** together to look like toadstools and stood them on a bed of

SCARY SPIDER

INGREDIENTS: one large green zucchini, salad dressing of your choice, one grape tomato, one yellow pepper

Have an adult help you cut the zucchini in half and roast it in the oven at 350 degrees Fahrenheit for ten to fifteen minutes, until it starts to brown. On a round plate, use the salad dressing to draw a spiderweb. When the zucchini is done, place one half in the center of the plate with a grape tomato on one end, creating the body and the head of the spider. Then cut eight thin slices of yellow pepper and lay four on each side of the zucchini to make "legs." Enjoy!

fresh basil. Violet, Elly, and Ryder made a **spinach-and-radish** quiche in the shape of a face. Craig, Ron, and Tanja made a scary-looking spider out of zucchini, yellow pepper slices, and grape tomatoes!

All of the teams did a fabumouse job, but Chef Crouton was especially impressed by what Colette and Ruby came up with. The two mouselets had prepared a checkerboard using pureed carrots and pureed zucchini! They had even made checkers out of carrot and zucchini slices.

"Sure as squeaking, there's plenty of imagination here at Mouseford!" Chef Crouton exclaimed. "However, Colette and Ruby have come up with a marvemousely creative dish that you makes you want to eat — and play! They are the winners of this round!"

A DIFFICULT
DECISION

By the end of the final round, all four teams were **TIED**, with one point apiece. Chef Crouton decided to take a break from filming the **show** so he could think over the situation.

As soon as Pam heard, she ran to Vince. "We're taking a break from the competition — how about renting some **scooters** and riding around the island?"

Vince squeaked with joy! He was thrilled to spend some time with his sister. She'd been so busy with the show they hadn't been able to go on any **ADVENTURES** together!

But when Vince arrived at the dorm to meet Pam, helmet in paw, Colette opened the door with a paw to her lips. "Pam just fell asleep — she was **exhausted**!"

Walking back to his room alone, Vince couldn't help thinking that maybe he had picked the **wrong** time to visit his sister. But Pam was so **busy** at Mouseford. Would there **ever** be a good time?

So Vince decided to change his flight and **HEAD BACK** to New York early the next morning. He didn't want to get in Pam's way, after all.

But when he went to his ꜱɪꜱᴛᴇʀ'ꜱ room to say good-bye, nobody was there.

"Are you looking for Pam?" someone asked from behind him. It was Shen — all better now! — who added, "Chef Crouton called her and all the other competitors back

to the studio. I'm HEADING there now, too!"

Vince didn't want to give Pam anything else to worry about, so he decided to just leave a good-bye note outside of her room, along with the gift he hadn't had a chance to give her. Crusty cat litter, he wished his sister weren't so busy!

TEAM LEADERS IN THE SPOTLIGHT!

In the meantime, the cameras started rolling again on the set of *Healthy Nibbles with Chef Crouton: Mouseford Special*. **CHEF CROUTON** had come up with a plan,

We'll have a tiebreaker!

which he explained to the contestants. "Since you all have the **SAME** score, I've decided to hold a tiebreaker, where the team leaders will FACE OFF. Each team will choose a leader to represent it and prepare the best healthy dish he or she can come up with — something **yummy** AND good for your tummy!"

What a mouserific idea!

The Green team announced that Craig would be their team leader. "He was the only one to figure out that one of the SECRET soup ingredients was shrimp," Tanja explained.

"Shen will be our team leader!" Colette declared, ignoring Ruby's FIERY look and turning to Shen instead. "You missed the last round because of your allergic reaction. It's only fair that you get a chance to show everyone what you can do!"

The Yellow team elected Elly as their team leader. She already had the perfect recipe in mind.

Finally, it was time for the Orange team to decide.

"Paulina and I choose you!" Nicky told Pam.

"Me? But . . . are you sure?" Pam asked,

tugging nervously on her whiskers.

"*PAW-SITIVELY!*" Paulina replied. "You're the only mouse here who took all of Chef Crouton's *lessons* and applied them to your own eating habits!"

Pam was a little worried — she wasn't really sure she would do such a fabumouse job, and she didn't want to let her friends

THE TEAM LEADERS

down. But Paulina's and Nicky's trusting smiles made her proud to represent the Orange team. She suddenly realized she already had the most important recipe of all right in her paws — the *friendship recipe*!

"Thank you, friends. I'll do my best! And you know what? I already know what I'm going to make!"

Pam scanned the audience for Vince, all while thinking about the dish she was going to prepare. "Wait, where's Vince?" she asked. "Maybe he doesn't know we're about to go back on the air? I have to find him!"

"No, Pam, you need to stay here and focus on the competition, " Nicky said firmly. "We'll go find Vince — RODent's HONoR!"

LOOKING FOR VINCE

Nicky and Paulina searched for Vince all over Mouseford. They figured maybe he had gone for a walk to enjoy the sunshine. But there was no sign of him anywhere!

"Could he be in the cafeteria, eating breakfast?" Paulina guessed.

"Or at the football field?" Nicky suggested.

Nicky had barely finished her sentence before she was **interrupted** by a familiar squeak. "We've been looking for you!"

It was Colette. She and Violet had noticed Nicky and Paulina leaving the set and decided to *FOLLOW* them.

They *joined* in the search for Vince, but he wasn't in the cafeteria or at the football field. **RATS!**

"Let's peek on the second floor of the dorm," Violet suggested. "Maybe he went to **LOOK** for Pam in her room."

The four of them didn't find Vince, but they did find a clue OUTSIDE of Colette and Pam's door.

"Look! A note and a package!" Paulina squeaked. The others all came running. "It's from Vince!"

"'Dear Pam,'" Nicky read. "'I decided to go back to **NEW YORK** earlier than planned. You're so busy, and I don't want to get IN THE WAY! I know the cooking competition is really important to you, and I wouldn't want to be a distraction. I hope I can visit again soon, when things aren't so fur-raisingly crazy!'"

The mouselets looked at one another in surprise. They were all afraid Vince had

misunderstood Pam's behavior!

They knew Pam well, so they knew **family** meant everything to her. She would never want Vince to feel like he was getting in her way!

"We have to rush to the port and **STOP** Vince!" Violet cried.

"Let's get our tails in gear," Colette agreed. "The morning ferry is about to leave!"

The four friends had to run as fast as their paws would take them, but when they reached the port they spotted Vince in the crowd of WAITING passengers. Colette, Paulina, Violet, and Nicky all breathed a big sigh of relief. WHEW!

"What are you all doing here?" Vince asked, surprised.

"We came to stop you from making an enormouse mistake!" Nicky replied.

The Thea Sisters explained to him that family was paw-sitively the most important thing to Pam — she never missed an opportunity to talk about her LARGE, warm family in New York.

"She was so excited to have you here!"

Violet squeaked. "PLEASE DON'T GO! She'll be heartbroken when she realizes you were feeling left out."

"Plus," Colette added, holding out Vince's gift, "you can't *LEAVE* without giving this to her yourself, **in the FUR**."

THE SPECIAL INGREDIENT

Back on set, Chef Crouton walked between the cooking stations, watching the team leaders kneading, blending, and slicing. Cheese niblets, they had learned **SO MUCH**!

Elly was focused and determined. She was making a light **lasagna** using whole-wheat pasta, homemade basil pesto, and fresh cheese.

Shen had just put his **watermelon** sorbet in the freezer, and he was now **CUTTING** the rind to use as a dish.

Craig was putting the final touches on his

PERFECT SANDWICH. It was a towering stack of whole-wheat bread, melted Swiss, lettuce, and grilled veggies!

Puzzled, Chef Crouton walked over to the Orange team's station. "Pam, where's your dish?"

"I'm all done!" Pam replied with a nervous smile. "My dish is in the oven — it will be ready in just a few minutes!"

Pam had been completely focused while she prepared her dish, but now she couldn't stop wondering where Vince and her friends had gone.

Pam was so preoccupied that she didn't even realize the round was over! Chef

Crouton asked each team leader to describe his or her RECIPE. Pam snapped back to reality when the chef called on her.

"Pamela, tell us about your DISH!"

Pam wished she could have waited for her brother to be there, but it was IMPAWSSIBLE. Her team was counting on her! With a **heavy heart**, she stepped over to the oven and pulled out her dream dish. As soon as she turned back toward the audience, however, she had a marvemouse SURPRISE — Vince and the Thea Sisters were suddenly sitting in the front row!

An enormouse smile LIT UP Pam's snout as she squeaked about her dish.

"My dream dish is pizza, not only because it's **delicious**, but mostly because every time I eat it, I feel like I'm at home in my family's **pizzeria**. It helps when I'm feeling homesick! So this is PIZZA THIRTEEN: a whole-wheat vegetable pizza. Each slice features fresh mozzarella and a different topping — the favorites of each of the thirteen mice in my family!"

The room filled with boisterous applause. After a moment, Chef Crouton declared, "The team that wins the last round, and therefore the cooking competition, is the Orange Team! With Pizza Thirteen, Pam prepared a healthy, tasty dish, with an extra helping of the most special ingredient — love!"

A PERFECT MOMENT

Thanks to Colette, Violet, Paulina, and Nicky, Vince had realized that he'd been wrong about Pam. But it was only when he heard Pam talk about her inspiration for PIZZA THIRTEEN that he was paw-sitively sure — nothing would ever replace their family in Pam's **heart**!

"Little sister, you were fabumouse!" Vince exclaimed, running to hug Pam with the Thea Sisters right on his tail.

"Yes," Paulina agreed. "You were mousetastic!"

"And Vince brought a very special gift as your prize!" Colette went on, winking at Vince.

As she unwrapped the gift, Pam's eyes

filled with tears. "Wow! This is the picture we took last summer at the amousement park!" She proudly showed the framed photo to her friends. "My whole family was there. This is **better than cheddar**! Thank you so much, Vince!"

Holding the 🄿🄸🄲🅃🅄🅁🄴 of her family

in her paws, surrounded by her brother and best friends, Pam felt like the **luckiest** mouse alive! She had a loving family and friends who always looked out for her. If that wasn't a recipe for happiness, Pam didn't know what was!

Only one thing was missing.

Hooray for pizza!

Tasty!

"Hey, how about a slice of Pizza Thirteen?"

Pam squeaked with a smile.

Don't miss any of these Mouseford Academy adventures!

#1 Drama at Mouseford

#2 The Missing Diary

#3 Mouselets in Danger

#4 Dance Challenge

#5 The Secret Invention

#6 A Mouseford Musical

#7 Mice Take the Stage

#8 A Fashionable Mystery

#9 The Mysterious Love Letter

#10 A Dream on Ice

#11 Lights, Camera, Action!

#12 Mice on the Runway

#13 Sea Turtle Rescue

#14 The Secret Notebook

#15 The Friendship Recipe

#16 The Royal Ball

Don't miss any of these exciting Thea Sisters adventures!

Thea Stilton and the Dragon's Code

Thea Stilton and the Mountain of Fire

Thea Stilton and the Ghost of the Shipwreck

Thea Stilton and the Secret City

Thea Stilton and the Mystery in Paris

Thea Stilton and the Cherry Blossom Adventure

Thea Stilton and the Star Castaways

Thea Stilton: Big Trouble in the Big Apple

Thea Stilton and the Ice Treasure

Thea Stilton and the Secret of the Old Castle

Thea Stilton and the Blue Scarab Hunt

Thea Stilton and the Prince's Emerald

Thea Stilton and the Mystery on the Orient Express

Thea Stilton and the Dancing Shadows

Thea Stilton and the Legend of the Fire Flowers

Thea Stilton and the Spanish Dance Mission

Thea Stilton and the Journey to the Lion's Den

**Thea Stilton and the
Great Tulip Heist**

**Thea Stilton and the
Chocolate Sabotage**

**Thea Stilton and the
Missing Myth**

**Thea Stilton and the
Lost Letters**

**Thea Stilton and the
Tropical Treasure**

**Thea Stilton and the
Hollywood Hoax**

**Thea Stilton and the
Madagascar Madness**

**Thea Stilton and the
Frozen Fiasco**

**Thea Stilton and the
Venice Masquerade**

And check out my fabumouse special editions!

THEA STILTON:
THE JOURNEY
TO ATLANTIS

THEA STILTON:
THE SECRET OF
THE FAIRIES

THEA STILTON:
THE SECRET OF
THE SNOW

THEA STILTON:
THE CLOUD
CASTLE

THEA STILTON:
THE TREASURE
OF THE SEA

THEA STILTON:
THE LAND OF
FLOWERS

Meet
CREEPELLA VON CACKLEFUR

Geronimo Stilton, have a lot of mouse friends, but none as **spooky** as my friend CREEPELLA VON CACKLEFUR! She is an enchanting and MYSTERIOUS mouse with a pet bat named **Bitewing.** YIKES! I'm a real 'fraidy mouse, but even I think CREEPELLA and her family are AWFULLY fascinating. I can't wait for you to read all about CREEPELLA in these a-mouse-ly funny and **spectacularly spooky** tales!

#1 The Thirteen Ghosts

#2 Meet Me in Horrorwood

#3 Ghost Pirate Treasure

#4 Return of the Vampire

#5 Fright Night

#6 Ride for Your Life!

#7 A Suitcase Full of Ghosts

#8 The Phantom of the Theater

#9 The Haunted Dinosaur

Be sure to read all my fabumouse adventures!

#1 Lost Treasure of the Emerald Eye

#2 The Curse of the Cheese Pyramid

#3 Cat and Mouse in a Haunted House

#4 I'm Too Fond of My Fur!

#5 Four Mice Deep in the Jungle

#6 Paws Off, Cheddarface!

#7 Red Pizzas for a Blue Count

#8 Attack of the Bandit Cats

#9 A Fabumouse Vacation for Geronimo

#10 All Because of a Cup of Coffee

#11 It's Halloween, You 'Fraidy Mouse!

#12 Merry Christmas, Geronimo!

#13 The Phantom of the Subway

#14 The Temple of the Ruby of Fire

#15 The Mona Mousa Code

#16 A Cheese-Colored Camper

#17 Watch Your Whiskers, Stilton!

#18 Shipwreck on the Pirate Islands

#19 My Name Is Stilton, Geronimo Stilton

#20 Surf's Up, Geronimo!

#21 The Wild, Wild West

#22 The Secret of Cacklefur Castle

A Christmas Tale

#23 Valentine's Day Disaster

#24 Field Trip to Niagara Falls

#25 The Search for Sunken Treasure

#26 The Mummy with No Name

#27 The Christmas Toy Factory

#28 Wedding Crasher

#29 Down and Out Down Under

#30 The Mouse Island Marathon

#31 The Mysterious Cheese Thief

Christmas Catastrophe

#32 Valley of the Giant Skeletons

#33 Geronimo and the Gold Medal Mystery

#34 Geronimo Stilton, Secret Agent

#35 A Very Merry Christmas

#36 Geronimo's Valentine

#37 The Race Across America

#38 A Fabumouse School Adventure

#39 Singing Sensation

#40 The Karate Mouse

#41 Mighty Mount Kilimanjaro

#42 The Peculiar Pumpkin Thief

#43 I'm Not a Supermouse!

#44 The Giant Diamond Robbery

#45 Save the White Whale!

#46 The Haunted Castle

#47 Run for the Hills, Geronimo!

#48 The Mystery in Venice

#49 The Way of the Samurai

#50 This Hotel Is Haunted!

#51 The Enormouse Pearl Heist

#52 Mouse in Space!

#53 Rumble in the Jungle

#54 Get into Gear, Stilton!

#55 The Golden Statue Plot

#56 Flight of the Red Bandit

Special Edition!
The Hunt for the Golden Book

#57 The Stinky Cheese Vacation

#58 The Super Chef Contest

#59 Welcome to Moldy Manor

Special Edition!
The Hunt for the Curious Cheese

#60 The Treasure of Easter Island

#61 Mouse House Hunter

#62 Mouse Overboard!

Special Edition!
The Hunt for the Secret Papyrus

#63 The Cheese Experiment

#64 Magical Mission

#65 Bollywood Burglary

Special Edition!
The Hunt for the Hundredth Key

#66 Operation: Secret Recipe

#67 The Chocolate Chase

MEET
Geronimo Stiltonord

He is a mouseking — the Geronimo Stilton of the ancient far north! He lives with his brawny and brave clan in the village of Mouseborg. From sailing frozen waters to facing fiery dragons, every day is an adventure for the micekings!

#1 Attack of the Dragons

#2 The Famouse Fjord Race

#3 Pull the Dragon's Tooth!

#4 Stay Strong, Geronimo!

#5 The Mysterious Message

#6 The Helmet Holdup

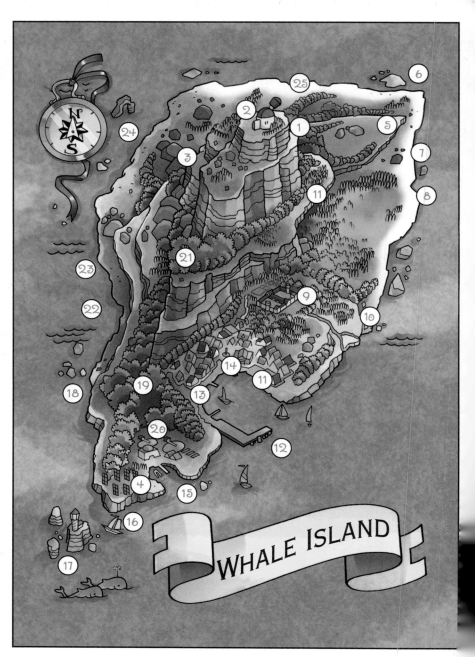

WHALE ISLAND

MAP OF
WHALE ISLAND

1. Falcon Peak
2. Observatory
3. Mount Landslide
4. Solar Energy Plant
5. Ram Plain
6. Very Windy Point
7. Turtle Beach
8. Beachy Beach
9. Mouseford Academy
10. Kneecap River
11. Mariner's Inn
12. Port
13. Squid House
14. Town Square
15. Butterfly Bay
16. Mussel Point
17. Lighthouse Cliff
18. Pelican Cliff
19. Nightingale Woods
20. Marine Biology Lab
21. Hawk Woods
22. Windy Grotto
23. Seal Grotto
24. Seagulls Bay
25. Seashell Beach

THANKS FOR READING, AND GOOD-BYE UNTIL OUR NEXT ADVENTURE!

Thea Sisters